A Random House PICTUREBACK®

# *The Best Time of Day*

*The*

Library of Congress Catalog Card Number: 77-91641.
ISBN: 0-394-83786-X (B.C.); 0-394-83799-1 (trade).
Manufactured in the United States of America.
A B C D E F G H I J    2 3 4 5 6 7 8 9 0

# Best Time of Day

by Valerie Flournoy    illustrated by George Ford

RANDOM HOUSE 🏠 NEW YORK

Sometimes William thinks early morning is the best time of day. When he hears his father's car drive away, he knows it is time to get up.

He climbs out of bed, puts on his bathrobe, and
hurries to wash his face and brush his teeth.

Today is a brand-new day!
William can hardly wait to get
downstairs and say "good morning"
to his mother. "Is breakfast ready?"
William asks.

William always helps at breakfast time.
He puts the silverware and dishes on the table
while Mother cooks.

William likes bacon and eggs for breakfast, or pancakes with lots of butter and syrup. But he doesn't like oatmeal. It's too lumpy. This morning Mother is making pancakes.

William feeds his goldfish breakfast, too. He takes the box marked FISH FOOD and sprinkles a little food on top of the water. Then William watches his fish swim to the top of the aquarium. *Gulp, gulp, gulp* — the food disappears.

William doesn't ever like to clean his room. Sometimes he hides his toys and dirty clothes in the closet or underneath his bed.

But Mother doesn't like it when she finds William's things aren't put away.

Then William has to clean his room again — while Mother watches.

When Mother goes to class, William
likes to go to the community center
with his babysitter.

He slides down the sliding board
with the other boys and girls
in the playground.

And sometimes William soars
through the air on the swing.
"Higher, higher!" he always says.

William likes playing with his friends Keith and Wayne.
But he doesn't always play nice. Sometimes he won't let
anyone else ride in the community center car. Keith gets
angry and Wayne starts to cry.

William's babysitter says if he won't share the car
with his friends she'll take him home.

Lunchtime means peanut butter
and jelly, and William loves
peanut butter and jelly.

He knows how to make his own
sandwich and pour himself a
glass of cold milk.

Today William drips jelly
on his shirt. "Uh-oh," he says.
"I'm in trouble now."

William doesn't think nap time is a good time of day. Most of the time, he doesn't like to take a nap at all. But after he's played very hard and his eyes are so heavy he can't keep them open, William curls up and takes a rest.

Sometimes William has to go to the doctor's office.
The doctor lets him listen to his own heartbeat
through a funny instrument called a stethoscope,
and the nurse usually gives him a lollipop.

But William doesn't like it
when the doctor sticks a needle
in his arm.

"This medicine will keep
you healthy," the doctor says.
But the needle makes William
cry anyway.

William often goes to the supermarket with his mother. He helps her pick out the things on the shopping list and holds the money tightly in his fist.

William doesn't open his hand until he gets to the check-out counter. Mr. Thompson counts out the change and tells William what a big boy he is getting to be.

Going visiting is always fun. William likes to visit his Aunt Debbie and her new baby.

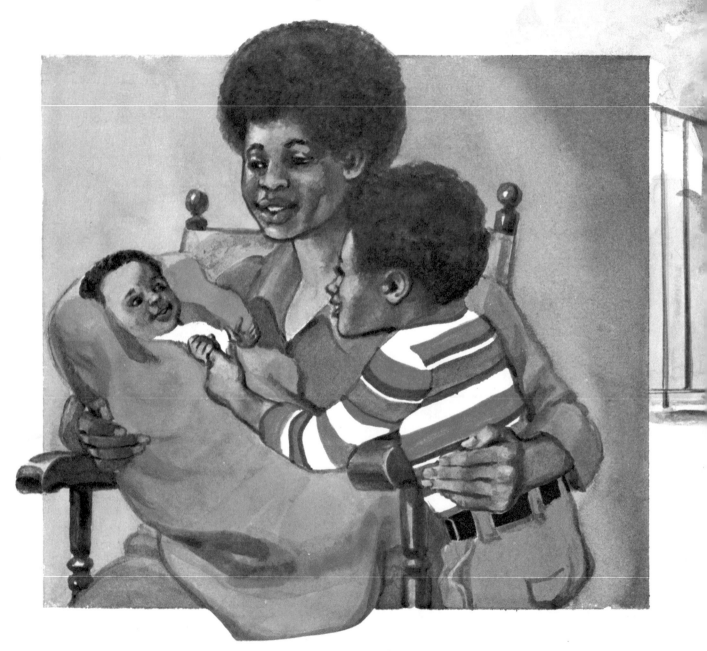

They take long walks together, and William pushes
the baby in her stroller. The cool breeze blows in their
faces and makes the baby laugh. William laughs, too.

William loves to stay with his grandparents when his parents
are away. Sometimes Aunt Debbie and the baby are there, too.
Everyone listens while William reads his grandpa a story.
Then Grandma hums a soft song until it's time to go to bed.

William likes to do all kinds of things. But he loves
one time of day more than any other.

It's not setting the table for breakfast, or feeding
his goldfish in the morning. And it certainly isn't
cleaning his room, or taking a nap, or going to the doctor's
office. It's not visiting Aunt Debbie and the baby, or
his grandparents, though he loves them very much.

William's favorite time of day is early evening. He listens until he hears a car in the driveway. He looks out the window and sees a big man walking toward the house.

"It's Daddy!" William calls. "Daddy's home!"

That is the best time of day.

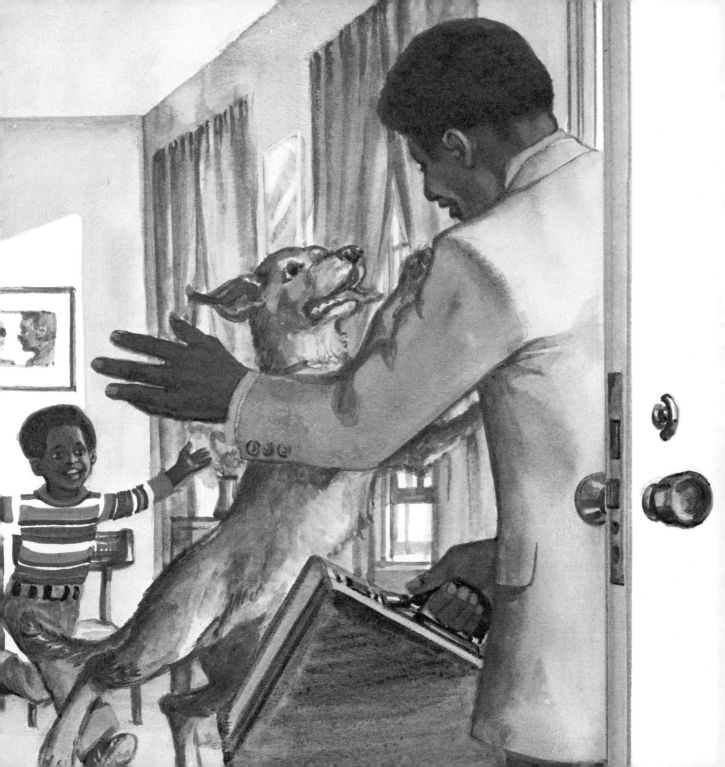

William and his father always play for a while until dinner is ready.

Just before bedtime, William and his mother and Daddy talk about their day.

At bedtime William usually calls for one more drink of water.
But what he really wants is a hug — the perfect end of a busy day.